D1247130

THE

ROBIN McKINLEY

STONE

Illustrated by JOHN CLAPP

FEY

HARCOURT BRACE & COMPANY

San Diego   New York   London

Library of Congress Cataloging-in-Publication Data

McKinley, Robin.

The stone fey/Robin McKinley; illustrated by John Clapp.

p.   cm.

Summary: Maddy, a young woman who runs sheep on her family farm,
develops an unusual relationship with an elusive mountain creature called a fey.

ISBN 0-15-200017-8

[1. Supernatural—Fiction.] I. Clapp, John, ill. II. Title.

PZ7.M1988St   1998

[Fic]—dc20   95-3915

First edition

A   C   E   F   D   B

Printed in Singapore

The paintings in this book were done in graphite and watercolor on cold-press watercolor paper.

The display type was designed by Judythe Sieck and inked by Barry Age.

The text type was set in Centaur by Thompson Type, San Diego, California.

Color separations by United Graphic Pte Ltd., Singapore

Printed and bound by Tien Wah Press, Singapore

This book was printed on totally chlorine-free Nymolla Matte Art paper.

Production supervision by Stanley Redfern and Pascha Gerlinger

Designed by Linda Lockowitz

To the memory of Littlejohn,
who should have had some sheep to herd

——R. M.

For my parents and friends,
for all their love and support

——J. C.

It would soon be too dark to see anything . . .

SHE WAS OUT NEAR TWILIGHT one evening, looking for a strayed lamb and muttering under her breath about the stupidity of sheep; truly they were the stupidest creatures ever created. It was a great misfortune that wool was so useful an item, and mutton so nourishing. Her dog, terribly embarrassed that he had not noticed the lamb's absence earlier, slunk along at her heels. "Anyone would think you went in fear of a beating," she said to him, and he flattened his ears humbly. She sighed. Aerlich was an admirable sheepdog, but he took himself very seriously.

It would soon be too dark to see anything, but a succulent young lamb would not survive the night in the wild rocky scree beyond the farm; if a folstza didn't get him, a yerig would. Damn. And she needed all her lambs; there had been several stillborns in her small flock this year, and none of the ewes had thrown twins; she was already short her usual market count.

Aerlich paused, raised his head, and pricked his ears. He tried to growl, or thought about growling, or started to growl and then changed his mind; dropped his head again; and looked confused.

Something had appeared from the twilight, from the low scrub trees, from the rocky foothills of the Horfels where they stood; something stood on the faint deer trail they had been following, and faced them, holding a lamb—her lamb—in his arms.

He walked toward them. The lamb seemed quite content where it lay cuddled next to his breast. Aerlich growled again, stopped again, sighed, and sat tightly down by her feet. She could feel how tense he was, for what came to them, cuddling their sleepy lamb, was not human. If he had turned away, tried to run; if the lamb had bleated or struggled, Aerlich would have been on him at once. Aerlich, who was afraid of almost everything, was fearless as a sheepdog. He had once almost gotten them both killed trying to take on a whole pack of yerig by himself, and she, with as little foresight as her dog, had gone to help him. They both still wore the scars, but the yerig hadn't been hungry enough to take the victory they could have had, and she and Aerlich had been permitted to save their sheep.

What walked toward them now walked silently, on bare feet; she stood her ground, but she found her knees were trembling. Aerlich pressed against her nearer knee as the walker drew close to them. He stopped only when he was an arm's-length away, so that he could hold the lamb out to her; and she, bemused, accepted it into her own arms. It gave a little grunt of annoyance at being so disturbed, but settled again straight away, its head on her shoulder, its stupid, gentle eye glazed with drowsy contentment.

He was just her height; she looked into black eyes, the iris as black as the pupil.

"Thank you," she said; her voice sounded so unnatural that Aerlich stirred, and growled again, audibly this time, but the half man before them never glanced at the dog. He looked into her eyes for a long moment, and her heart beat in her throat; and then he smiled, or only seemed to smile as the night shadows moved across his face; and then he turned away, and disappeared again into the fast-lowering twilight.

IT WAS DEEP DARK by the time she got back to the farm. Partly from weariness, partly from the dark, partly from bewilderment at the strange meeting with the creature that had given her back her lamb, she stumbled several times. The successive jerks in their progress eventually woke her prodigal. It noticed perhaps that it had missed its dinner, and grew irritable. Aerlich, trotting at her side, looked up at her anxiously as it began to kick and baa aggrievedly. "If you don't be good, I'll make you walk," she said to it, and tripped over another rough spot in the ground.

The bereaved mother had made herself hysterical over her loss, and having gotten so far into her hysteria it took a while before she could be convinced that she was no longer bereaved. The animals were all restless with her fretting, and by the time the barn was quiet and the doors shut for the night, she and Aerlich were both exhausted. She leaned against the barn door and looked at the sky; it was vaster here, she believed, than anywhere else on earth, and she had never had any desire to discover empirically if this were true or not.

. . . it was vaster here, she believed, than anywhere else on earth . . .

The stars were coming out, white and shining, over the crowns of the Horfels; there were the merest wisps of clouds drifting, high and far away, across the midnight blue: fair weather again tomorrow. It was a windless night, and almost silent. Her shepherd's ear—and Aerlich's relaxed body sprawled beside her—told her that none of the small rustlings she heard were dangerous to sheep.

A breath of cooking smell crept to her from the farmhouse; dear Ifgold, she'd told him she might be out late after her lost lamb, though he'd only scowled. It was almost worth the aggravation—at least since she'd found it, or it had been found for her—not to cook dinner an extra night, and Ifgold was never mean about return favors.

She sighed, and Aerlich raised his head from the ground and looked up at her, and stirred his plumy tail when she smiled at him, but it was only a very little stir, because, after all, he had not found the lamb himself. Aerlich's mother had been one of the merriest beings she had ever known; how could such a charming mother have given birth to so solemn a son? But he had inherited her sheep sense, which was the important thing.

The food smells tickled her and her stomach rumbled, but she wasn't ready to go inside yet. She slid down the barn door and sat on the ground next to her dog, who looked at her earnestly a moment, and then, tentatively, put his chin on her knee. His mother would have jumped onto her lap at once, and then scrabbled up to put her forepaws on her mistress's shoulders. On a whim she leaned over and picked Aerlich up as she would a lamb, and set him on her lap. He started to scramble off again in alarm—whether it was his dignity or hers that he felt had been outraged she couldn't begin to guess—and paused with his hindquarters still across her thighs. He bent his head around and looked seriously into her face, and visibly changed his mind. He didn't fit in her lap any more than his mother had, but he scooted around again, slid down her outstretched legs, let his forepaws trail over her hips, and rested his head on her stomach. He half shut his eyes and sighed profoundly.

She looked up at the sky again, her fingers trailing through Aerlich's silky hair. She had lived in this farmhouse all her life. When her mother, Thassie, had married Tim, she had brought him here to the farm, where she and her mother before her had lived all their lives. Tim had contentedly built a short wing off the kitchen for his jewelry-making, and took his pieces to town occasionally when his wife or his eldest daughter went on market-day. But the outside world didn't impinge too much on Tim; she was surprised he'd bestirred himself enough even to marry her bustling mother. And while Thassie was Mother, Tim had always been Tim, even to the littlest of them.

He was good with babies—better than Mother, really—and was happy to nurse the very young ones while Mother tended her vegetables; but as soon as they were old enough to start learning their letters and doing useful chores, he lost interest. Ifgold had said to her once, sadly, that he thought Tim had to remember his name every time he looked at him, his only son.

"He's that way with all of us, you know," she said, offering what comfort she could.

"I know," Ifgold said slowly. "I don't know why it still bothers me.... At least you have market-day; he has to recognize you then."

She smiled faintly. "Not true. He looks surprised when I come to his stall and tell him it's time to go home. It takes him a minute to realize I have the right to say it."

If anyone was to see strange things in their Hills, it should be Tim, dreamy Tim, who made such necklaces that one was even bought by a sola to give his lady in the great City of the king. His daughter was only a shepherd.

She knew what it was that she had seen; she remembered her grandmother's tales, for her grandmother was a little less matter-of-fact than her mother. Perhaps there was a little more of Tim in her than she realized, for she remembered those tales of the wild things that lived in their Hills far more vividly than a shepherd need; there was even supposed to be a wizard who had lived for thousands of years somewhere to the south of them. But she had spent too much time alone with her dog, wandering the low wild foothills, not to know that there were creatures that lived there she could not call by name; things besides the yerig and the folstza, the small shy orobog, the sweet-singing britti; things that were not birds or beasts, or lizards or fish or spiders.

Things like what had brought her back her lamb. She recognized him from one of her grandmother's stories: he was a stone fey. They were shorter and burlier than the other feys, with broad shoulders and heavy bones; in her childhood she had imagined them as shambling and clumsy, but she knew now it was not so. It was his skin that

. . . things that were not birds or beasts, or lizards or fish or spiders.

had told her for sure, for his skin was grey, the grey of rocks, and yet it was obvious—as her grandmother's story had told her it was obvious—that it was not the color of ill-health, and there was a rose-quartz flush across his cheekbones.

The smell of dinner would not let her sit any longer. She patted Aerlich and said, "We must go." He skittered off her lap at once and grovelled, certain that he wasn't supposed to have been there in the first place, and she laughed. "You are impossible," she told him. "Come along; you must be hungry too."

Ifgold looked up from his work at once when he heard the door; Tim, staring dreamily into the fire, didn't look up at all. Thassie didn't raise her eyes from the piecework on her lap, but she got that listening look on her face that all her children knew well. Berry sat frowning over a book at the end of the long kitchen table; she looked up briefly with a smile for her big sister as sweet and vague as Tim's, and then went back to her book. The littlest ones were already in bed.

"I found the lamb," she said.

"Good," said Ifgold.

Thassie smiled. Her tidy fingers seemed to spin the thread through the neat hems and corners; between her quilts and her vegetables the farm needed no extra income. Her daughter's sheep were her own idea. The farm had had sheep in her grandmother's day, but Thassie was an only child, and it had taken her brood to begin to push the farm's productivity back up to what it had been. But Thassie was firm about where her children's profits went: Ifgold and Berry needed more schooling than the small village school could give them, and everything that could be spared from seed and fence posts and shingles and sheep-dip went into the small but plump linen bag in the bottom of the wardrobe in Thassie and Tim's bedroom. Kitchet complained regularly that she had picked enough vegetables and dug enough holes and pulled enough weeds to have earned three ponies and she only wanted one, but no one stood up long to Thassie. Or almost no one. Her eldest daughter smiled a little wryly.

Ifgold would be going to a school in the south soon, and she would miss him, not only for the dinners he cooked out of turn, but because he was the only one of them all she could talk to. Mother was inimically businesslike, dispensing sympathy as neatly as she added up columns of figures; and Berry was as impossible to talk to as Tim was, or nearly; and the others were too young.

She bent to kiss her mother and then Tim. "Lamb?" he said.

"I did tell him," Thassie said.

She shrugged. "Lamb. One strayed. I was lucky to find it."

Tim, who barely recognized his daughter from the rest of the people on market-day, heard something in her voice, and looked up at her almost sharply; but Ifgold said innocently, "Luck indeed. But you could use a little." Ifgold knew—unlike Tim—that ewes should have twins sometimes, and that none of hers had this season. Thassie murmured something in agreement, and Ifgold got up from his books—Berry took the opportunity to reach across the table and grab whatever it was he had been reading—and dipped up some of his stew on a plate. She sat down gratefully and let him serve her.

He put a bowl on the floor as well for Aerlich. "Everyone else has eaten." Looking across the table he said in sudden outrage, "You're supposed to be doing your schoolwork!" He glowered, but Berry ignored him, absorbed in the stolen book.

Curious, she reached out and delicately raised the book in Berry's hands till she could read the spine: *Tales of the Feys.* She dropped it as if it burnt her fingers, and Berry, startled, said, "I have done my schoolwork."

Embarrassed, she muttered, "I'm sorry. I didn't mean to disturb you."

From the fireside, Thassie said, "Finish the chapter, Berry, and off to bed with you."

Berry left, grumbling, and Ifgold reclaimed his book. He turned it over to look at the back, and then looked measuringly at his older sister; but she refused to meet his eyes, concentrating on her food. "I can at least do the washing-up," she said.

"I was hoping you'd say that," Ifgold said.

Tim drifted over to dry the dishes for her, but she had to put them away if they were to go anywhere that anyone could find them again. It was not usual for him to do any of the homely chores unless they involved a hammer or saw, and she had not liked the sudden intent look he'd given her when she'd come in.

"The lamb," he said, as she hung the dishrag over the edge of the sink and prepared to blow out the lamp that hung beside it. "It was all right when you found it?"

"Yes," she said. "I—" She wanted to tell him about the stone fey; Tim might even understand. But something stopped her words. She stood staring into the sink a moment, but she did not see the sink or the rag or her white-knuckled hands; she saw a grey-skinned face framed in black hair, and the intense black eyes that had looked into her own. When she looked up, Tim was still watching her with the same sharpness so unlike him. "I think I'm just tired," she said.

She climbed the stairs to her bedroom. She had fought and won the right to have a private bedroom; she was the eldest, and earned the most money—after Thassie—and she had to keep strange hours during lambing season. In exchange her room was the smallest, no more than a closet with a crack of window, but she didn't mind; it had a door on it that closed her in and the rest of the world out. Except Aerlich, who slept on the narrow bit of rug between her bed and the wall.

She hung her clothes on their peg, and leaned her elbows a moment on the windowsill—which was just about two elbows wide—and looked up again at her Hills. Even on cloudy nights she could look out her window and see in her mind's eye what the weather obscured; but tonight it wasn't necessary. Even the last faint shreds of cloud had left, and the sky was ablaze with stars. She wondered where the stone fey was, if he looked at the sky before he slept; if he slept out-of-doors or in some secret, stony cavern; if he slept. Perhaps at night he walked far over the Hills on his bare silent feet; perhaps he had been walking far this evening, when he found her lamb, and would never come this way again. She shook her head.

When she had trouble sleeping, she counted over in her mind

. . . and the sky was ablaze with stars.

the little pile of coins that was going to buy her own farm someday soon, the farm for herself and Donal; a little pile that when she had first wrested the right to it from her mother was small enough to fit under her thin mattress without discomfort. But it had grown bigger, slowly, and it lived now in another linen bag, smaller than the one in her parents' wardrobe, in a spare boot under her bed. With Donal's little pile they would soon be able to buy what they needed to settle on the bit of land they had chosen—that she had found one day, wandering far afield with her sheep—not too far from here, not so far that the Hills and the sky would look different from their new windows.

Donal had hired himself out this year as a logger, far away in the western mountains, near the mines; he had been gone only three months, and she would not see him again for another nine. She missed him bitterly, for while their parents' farms were far enough apart that they did not see each other daily nor at busy times even weekly, they had grown up together, had been good friends since she was eleven and he was ten and a half, when she'd met him at a market-day, trying to steal one of her first sheep. He hadn't realized it was one of hers—he said—and by the time they had it sorted out (involving several bruises and one black eye—his) they were well on their way to becoming excellent friends. But as friendship had turned to love and thoughts of a life together and a farm of their own, they had discussed their chances, over and over again. She had finally, reluctantly, agreed to his plan to go away; his salary for a year was worth three times what she could earn by her flock—and probably more than that, this year.

She might not have had the strength of will, finally, to push it to the end with her mother, had she not had Donal to help her. Donal, youngest of six as she was eldest, was as determined as she, for perhaps precisely the opposite reasons, to have a life independent of his family—and he had had little choice, for the fourth and fifth children had already been afterthoughts, and there was little left for the sixth but kindness. Donal was the last person to be willing to plunge himself into another overflowing family, another family where he would always feel slightly superfluous. . . . She had wondered more than once if that had not been part of his initial attraction for her: someone to remind her when she wavered of how splendid it would be to be making their own fresh, new, individual mark on a piece of land unaccustomed to human feet and hands, and ploughs and scythes.

The only time she had ever seen her mother upset to the point of complete physical stillness was when she told her that she and Donal wanted their own farm. The eldest daughter had always brought her husband here; for generations it had been that way, back almost to Aerin's day, so her grandmother had said. She didn't know why it meant so much to her that she should leave, that her land should be new land, land that had not been farmed for generations of her own blood; perhaps she hadn't known till she met Donal. But that wasn't true, for she hadn't known Donal when Berry was born, and she was glad even then that there was another daughter, that even if it wouldn't be the eldest daughter, there would be another girl to grow up and take Thassie's place on the farm.

It wouldn't be Berry, though. Berry would be a scholar, or perhaps a teacher; she could hardly weed. Sometimes the little ones were a nuisance, but at least they provided three more girls, and Lonnie already was a passionate farmer.

But tonight she was too tired to think, and there seemed to be a cloud over her mind that was more than just tiredness; and the knowledge of the contents of a spare boot under the bed did not cheer her, nor the consciousness that every night was one day sooner that she would see Donal again give her any pleasure. She went to bed and fell asleep at once.

SHE SAW THE STONE FEY again only a sennight later. Since she had a smaller flock this year, she had taken the opportunity to range a little farther than she usually did—which was how she almost lost a lamb—looking for new pasture. Their country was stony, and all the local farmers with livestock were perennially occupied with keeping them fed. Her and Donal's farm would be little different; nowhere near the Hills was there rich land, but the Hills were the Hills. In the south, it was said, the trees were so lush they covered the sky in some places, and they could even grow oranges; but the Hills were her flesh and bone.

Her mother's farm was the farthest out. In Dockono, on market-day, she was the only one who came from the east. There was one other farmer whose land lay in as inhospitable a spot, to the north of her, and several from the south, but most of the farms lay west. It was a joke among those who met on the market-day streets that her farm and Nerra's must be blessed by the mountain wizard, for there was no other reason for there to be farms there at all.

Her and Donal's valley lay even farther away from the market at Dockono than her mother's farm, but it would be worth it for her, living in the Hills instead of only in their shadow; and by its individual geography its land was a little more arable than much of what lay near it, which pleased Donal. It had been in a year of drought that she'd found it; she'd had a small flock that year too, even smaller than this year, and even so she had had to range far, often gone from home for several nights together, to find enough fodder for her growing lambs.

But she had no drought as excuse this year. After she lost the lamb she should perhaps have gone back to her usual ways. But she didn't. She told herself that she would be extra watchful; she knew that Aerlich, still smarting in shame, was being extra watchful; and she told herself further that there was indeed no reason that her mother's farm did thrive—had thriven for several hundred years—and that if she could find new pasturage she should. For Lonnie's sake, perhaps, or Kitchet's. Kitchet liked animals better than vegetables too, and might want to have sheep. She did not think of the stone fey. So she told herself.

But she was not surprised when she saw him. She looked up, one afternoon, and he was sitting on a rock; near her, but not too near. She had no idea if he had been there all along, or if he had only just arrived, stepping so softly that even Aerlich—intent, at present, in facing down one of the oldest ewes, who felt she was beyond having to pay attention to a young whippersnapper of a sheepdog—had not noticed him; or if he had materialized out of air, or out of the rock he sat on.

He turned his head slowly to meet her gaze. He did not look surprised; he did not look anything at all. He merely looked back at her as she looked at him. The angles of his face cast queer, inhuman shadows over his stone-grey features, and his black eyes gave her no clue of what he might be thinking.

She dropped her eyes first; then, remembering herself, glanced over to see if Aerlich needed any help with his ewe. He did not. She did not want to look up at the fey again—they were on a hill, and he sat a little above her—but her eyes were drawn to him in spite of herself. How often did a mortal see a fey, after all, particularly a stone fey, who was supposed to be the shyest of all the feys? Why should she not look?

He was still looking down at her, and she felt an unaccustomed flush rising to her face. Should she say something? Could she just get up and leave? Aerlich would justifiably feel put-upon if, just as he got the herd settled for the day, she decided to move. She found, suddenly, that she was sitting uncomfortably, and had to rearrange herself. But the stone she was on obstinately remained uncomfortable, and at last she got up and found another rock, higher on the hillside. When she glanced at the fey again he was still there and still watching her, but she was now even with him. No closer, but she did not have to look up anymore.

But she was not surprised when she saw him.

"What is your name?"

The sound of his voice startled her, as if a stone had spoken; yet her grandmother's tales had informed her that feys did speak when they chose to. She blinked at him while her surprise subsided; it was the choosing that startled her, not the speaking, although his voice was not, somehow, what she would have expected. A stone fey should have a deep, harsh voice, a rumbling, stony voice; his voice was none of these things.

"Maddy," she said.

Silence fell. She stared out over her herd. They were grazing across a little plateau, and the Hill fell away below them as it rose at her back. When she looked for the fey again, he was gone.

TWO DAYS LATER she found an *M* in a beautiful mosaic of shimmering greys, nestled at the threshold of her sheep barn. No one ever came to the barn but herself and Aerlich; she cleaned it herself, and even replaced fallen shingles herself. She would far rather shovel sheep dung than ever come near a seed or a plough; her mother's other children could help her there. Hating vegetable duty was how she got started on sheep.

She saw the stones gleaming from the ground even as the sheep pattered over them and disappeared into the twilight inside, milling and protesting as they felt obliged to do each evening. Aerlich got them neatly into their pen and waited for her to close the gate and bestow upon him the words of praise he deserved. He looked around, astonished at her absence. She was standing by the outer door, staring down. He whined, a tiny, questioning whine, and her head snapped up. She came inside, and closed the gate, and told Aerlich he was the finest sheepdog in Damar. He looked up into her face worriedly, however, even as his tail dutifully wagged, for her voice lacked conviction.

She went back outside, Aerlich at her heels, and looked at the shimmering grey stones again. They were both subtle and conspicuous; the gleam of the grey looked as if it were only a trick of the light, as if at just a slightly different time of day they would not show at all. They looked, most particularly, like things of twilight, like the uneasy ghosts one was supposed to be able to see only during that greyest of daylight; as if, when the sun set, they would fall back into being pebbles of no particular heritage and in no particular order. They were set so perfectly into the low stone-flagged ramp at the door of the barn that they looked as if they had been there always, though she knew they had not. They had not been there even so recently as that morning—and yet the barn was in clear sight of the house and most of the fields around it. How—?

Staring at the silver *M* was making her head ache. It lay just where she had sat, Aerlich in her lap, the evening she had lost the lamb, and had it found for her.

There was nothing to do; nothing to say. She went indoors to start dinner.

SHE SAW HIM AGAIN the next day. He seemed to be waiting for her; and yet she had not known, till she arrived at the little half valley on a knee of one of the foothills, that it would look good to her, and she would decide to stay.

Aerlich happily began to dispose of the sheep as suited him, and she flopped onto the ground. It was a good thing she raised her sheep primarily for their fleece; they were doing far too much walking, lately, to make them at all appetizing as mutton. Even the lambs must be getting thin and stringy. She watched while several of them at once sprang straight into the air, as young sheep will do, coming down again in a series of more or less graceful arcs, all now facing in different directions. They then pelted off, whichever way they were headed, apparently for no more reason than the pleasure of doing something dumb so often gives sheep of any age. Even a year ago such behavior still occasionally made Aerlich slightly hysterical, when he wasn't yet entirely accustomed to being the only sheepdog, and was first learning to do without his mother's somewhat overbearing direction. Maddy had had to help him sometimes, setting an example of placid resignation to the whimsies of their charges. Aerlich knew all about this sort of thing now, and was proud that he was in charge alone. The look of weary acquiescence on his face as he trotted off to head the wanderers back toward the flock again was a precise canine version of Maddy's own expression under similar circumstances.

She started to laugh, and from nowhere, in this wild place, she had the feeling she was being watched. She swallowed her laughter and looked around, and there he was, sitting on a rock near her as he had sat on another rock in another stretch of rough Hill-grass a few days before. Perhaps he spends all his days sitting on rocks in the foothills, she thought light-headedly; and picked herself up from her sprawl on the ground, and tried to sit with dignity. But she wasn't used to having to do anything with reference to dignity (except Aer-lich's) when she was out with her sheep, and she scowled and fidgeted, and eventually got to her feet and went toward her unexpected visitor—except, she thought, I suppose I'm his unexpected visitor. I really have no reason at all to be coming so far. . . .

She paused a few steps from his rock, first startled by her own presumption and then held by the thought that he might run away from her, like a stzik or deer or any wild thing; or turn into a rock, or vanish, or whatever the feys did. She looked into his face, timidly, and his eyes looked back at her, as inscrutable as any deer's. She did not receive the impression that her arrival was unexpected; rather, and for no good reason, except for the patient, quiet grace of his sitting and the slow way he turned his head to follow her with his eyes, that he had been expecting her for quite some time, and that she was late. Her stomach felt funny, and she decided to sit down where she was.

She wasn't prepared for him to get up from his rock and come so near to her that the little breeze of his motion brushed her face. He sat down beside her, and she tried to look at the ground around her feet, at the small rocks, spotted or plain, rough or smooth, at the grasses, short and sharp and yet a hundred different shades of green; but she saw nothing, for while her eyes looked her mind was wholly taken up with the sound of his breathing.

He smelled of green things, of the sorts of green things that grow in still, shady places, of mosses and ferns, with a background sharpness like a stream-washed rock, or herbs trod underfoot. It was a cool sort of smell, and she wanted to reach out for him, to see if his skin was cool to the touch; and then she wanted merely to touch him, for any reason whatsoever, and she clasped her hands tightly together, and stared miserably at her lap. He turned toward her and breathed something that might have been her name, and she raised her shoulders as if against a blow; and then felt his fingers, their touch only a little cooler than her own, on the nape of her neck, stroke up to her hairline, run along the curve of her jaw, and turn her face toward his.

Going home that night, she had little idea of where she was or where she was going; the sun was still in her eyes, the feel of his black hair and smooth grey skin under her fingers, the taste of his mouth in hers. She even thought she might jump straight into the air for no reason, and dash off in whatever direction she found herself in when she came down again, only for the pleasure of doing something dumb. When Aerlich had brought his mistress and his sheep safely home, she blinked up at the barn for a minute as if she didn't recognize it; and then she had to think for another minute to remember how to lift the bar down and open the doors.

THERE WERE MORE *M*s wound around the stones of the little hard-packed yard in front of the sheep barn over the next few weeks. They twined together like vines, like the tiny stitches of her mother's quilting; they seemed to make a larger pattern she could never quite grasp.

He smelled of green things . . .

And they seemed to say her name aloud to her when she stepped over them, echo her name under the small sheep hoofs, murmur her name after her as she walked away. In the evenings, the sheep safely penned for the night, she wanted to pause at the edge of the ramp, to listen to the whispering she might or might not be imagining; but Aerlich no longer enjoyed lingering anywhere in the barn's vicinity, and he would trot determinedly toward the farmhouse, his white tail-tip gleaming in the gathering twilight. He'd pause about halfway and turn, his white chest shining at her, though she could not see the reproachful look in his eyes; and she would pull herself away with a sigh, and follow him.

She tried to tease him about being overanxious for his supper, but he only looked at her sidelong, and she realized, for the first time in the four years of his life, that he did have a sense of humor; that he had teased her with his earnestness as she teased him for it—and she missed it now, because he would no longer play. He worried about her as he worried about his sheep, harried her as best he could for her own good—and, she thought, no longer credited her with much intelligence. She started to get angry with him one evening for this, and then realized how idiotic it was, to yell at your sheepdog for disapproving of your private life; perhaps she didn't entirely know what she was doing.

And yet she had always known exactly what she was doing; as the eldest of six children it was a central fact of her sanity, if not her survival. She always knew what she was doing, and she made her choices clearheadedly.

She grew vague with her family, more like Tim or Berry than

Ifgold or Thassie. She was asked, finally, if she were ill—after several conversations had stopped when she entered the room. She smiled, a smile they seemed not to like, and said that she was not. But Ifgold and her mother each asked her again, separately, drawing her aside, as if she might admit to something if she were alone. But she shook off their hands and their prying questions; she was not sick, and nothing else was any of their business. Even Tim asked her, one evening when she had come in particularly late and had had no reason to tell for it.

This at last made her angry, and she said sharply, "I am not ill. Do I look ill?" Aerlich crept away from her and disappeared behind Tim's chair. Tim was staring at her, a wrinkle between his brows that she couldn't remember ever having seen there before, and his eyes seemed darker than usual as he watched her, and she had the unpleasant feeling that since he looked at any of his children so rarely, perhaps when he did look at them he could see more. She turned abruptly away, and her mother was just at her shoulder, and laid a hand across her forehead. She started to jerk away, and then sighed and stood still.

"No," Thassie said. "You don't look ill, and I don't believe you have any fever. But you don't look like Maddy either."

"She looks haunted," Berry said. "Maybe she has a—"

"Hush," their mother said, fiercely for her. "Hush."

"It's what Grandmother would have said," Berry persisted. "You remember, her story about cousin whatever, third cousin forty times removed or something, Regh her name was? She went too far into the Hills to gather herbs, and—"

"Berry," said Tim, and Berry stopped in shock. She looked at her father with an expression suitable to one who has just heard a piece of furniture speak and give orders.

"I don't care what your grandmother would have said," Thassie said, and the tone of voice was so odd that Maddy was almost drawn back from wherever she'd wandered, these last weeks, to ask her mother if she were telling the truth. But she didn't.

"All I care is that she stop burning dinner," said Igard, one of the little ones. "You used to be able to trust Maddy. But she's as bad as Berry now."

"I don't burn dinner," Berry said irritably. "Hardly ever."

"Only about once a week," Igard said doggedly. "And you only have to cook once a week."

"That's enough of that," Thassie said.

"Yes, but—"

"Enough."

Silence fell, and Maddy permitted herself to wonder if she had changed so much. There was the way Aerlich watched her, even as her family did, unhappily; and the sheep began to shy away from her hands, which had never happened before. She did most of her own doctoring; she had to. The nearest healer who knew as much about sheep as she did lived on the other side of Dockono and by the time he got to the farm, or she got to him, it was often too late. She had an assortment of nasty little bottles and jars for most common ailments, and she knew how to pin a sheep in almost any position to get at whatever portion of its anatomy she needed to get at (with occasional help from Ifgold); but lately they seemed to flinch away from her in a way that had little to do with ordinary sheeply brainlessness.

That night when she went to bed she sat down on the floor and put her arms around Aerlich. He pulled his head free to lick her face—sadly, she thought, almost as if he were saying good-bye. "Is it truly so terrible?" she said. "It doesn't mean anything—I'm still Maddy. I *am* still Maddy. And it will all be over soon. I know it will be over soon." She shivered as she said that and put her face down on Aerlich's shoulder, and he sat very still, pressed up against her.

SHE ASKED HER FEY what his name was and he told her, Fel. She asked him if he had parents, brothers and sisters; he said he did, but he preferred solitude and saw them seldom; he did not volunteer any more. She wondered if all stone feys were solitary, or if he was unusual, but she did not ask him. She did not know what she might ask him, and feared to anger him; it was too important, too desperately important, that she be permitted to go on seeing him.

He never smiled when he saw her; her heart always paused, just for the moment when their eyes first met, in the hope that he would; and then, disappointed but obedient, took up its patient work again. She remembered that he never smiled only so long as it took him to come to her and put his arms around her; and then it no longer mattered, and till the afternoon, when she had to take her sheep home, it did not matter, till the next day.

He told her the fey names of different rocks and herbs; stone feys did not care much for trees or large animals, but they had names for each stage in a fern's life, and for the individual flavors of different waters, dependent on what minerals were dissolved in them and what plants might trail their leaves through them. Through him she saw her Hills as she had never seen them, and loved them as she had never loved them; but this new love had an ache in it. He smiled sometimes, briefly, over his rocks and ferns, but his eyes were always calm. He showed her how to walk quietly in the woods, for there were woods higher up on the sides of the Hills, and as the season progressed she found herself drawn higher and higher; and he taught her to move secretly even through the lower lands where there was little but rock and scree.

Or at least he taught her as much as he could; she was aware that she was not a very good pupil, however hard she tried. He did not scold her, any more than he praised her, or than he smiled at her. But she did not quite dare ask him about this either—even to ask him why he taught her. It was perhaps simply that what she offered him was enough—or so she told herself. What her sheep offered her was enough too, because she knew they were sheep.

She left the sheep-tending to Aerlich, who was perfectly competent to do it; and fortunately they did not run into any more yerig. But when, occasionally, during the days, she checked to see that Aerlich was still in command, she often caught him looking back at her with a puzzled, lonesome gaze that irritated her; what was a sheepdog for but to take care of sheep? He and Fel ignored each other; politely but implacably.

They never arranged to meet, but when she set out in the morning she seemed to know which way to go; and once they'd climbed

Through him she saw her Hills as she had never seen them . . .

well away from the farm she began to look eagerly around each bend in the path and over each boulder for him to appear. Occasionally it was a long time before she saw him, and she would go on, faster and a little faster, and a little faster yet, her breath coming a little too quickly for the climb, and the sheep beginning to protest the hurrying, till he did appear. And occasionally she did not get back home till after dark, which was foolish of her, for it was tricky enough to keep the sheep together and aimed in the right direction in daylight; and she dared not lose even one this year, for the sake of her farm. Her and Donal's farm. Her mind shied away from thoughts of Donal, though she preserved memory of him carefully, like an heirloom quilt in an old wooden chest, dried flowers tucked in its folds; something she wanted kept near her, something she might want to take out and shake free, and use, sometime in the future; just not right now.

And Ifgold was no longer there to cook for her when she was late. She had forgotten that he was to leave so soon; or perhaps more time had passed than she realized. Ifgold had tried the hardest to talk to her in the first weeks of her meetings with Fel, but she had told him that she had nothing to say, and smiled her new, dreamy smile; and then, when he persisted, she grew short with him, and began to avoid him. And then it was too late, for he was leaving.

"Will you write to me?" he said, a little desperately.

"Of course," she said, but they both knew she lied.

Ifgold shook his head. "I don't know what to do," he said, and his voice cracked; but he was still at an age when boys' voices do sometimes crack, and his eldest sister patted him on the shoulder and told him not to worry. His face crumpled like a much younger child's, and he turned away from her. Thassie was taking him to Dockono in the wagon, since he was lugging a box of his precious books with him, where he would meet with one other southbound scholar, that they might travel together. Ifgold turned once, when he was seated in the wagon; Maddy raised her hand in a final farewell, and he, reluctantly, raised his hand in response.

She almost ran up the Hills that day, for waiting to see her brother off had made her late getting started; and a few days later, when she took the early lambs to market, she failed to get as good a price for them as she should have, because she could not concentrate on her bargaining.

One of the nights that she should have made dinner she got back very late to be greeted by a furious Berry, who'd been impressed into duty in her absence—and who had contrived that there should not be enough dinner left for the latecomer. Maddy had to do with bread and apples, which wasn't nearly enough. As she bit slowly into her third apple, it occurred to her suddenly that she missed Ifgold. She had been thinking that she might justly complain to Thassie about Berry's behavior; she always paid back a dinner out of turn, and after a long day following sheep, she needed a hot supper, especially since her noon meal was always cold. It used to be that she took a tinderbox with her occasionally, and something that wanted cooking; Aerlich particularly liked those days. But Fel shied away from fires and hot food, and so she had not done so for a long time.

She took a second bite of the apple. But it probably wasn't worth complaining about; very little seemed to be worth much lately, except counting the hours till she saw Fel again. Funny about missing Ifgold; he was only her brother.

That night she dreamed, terribly, of Donal. She dreamed that he was caught under a falling tree, and he held his hands out to her, and called her, weeping, to help him; but Fel was waiting for her, if not around this bend in the path, then around just this next one. . . . She woke up, but the tears on her face were her own. It was still deep night. She crept to her windowsill, but there was no space to lean her elbows anymore, for she put the pebbles and small stones that she found in Fel's company there, to remind her of him during those long hours they were parted; and she drew back now as if they might burn her.

"We will not go high into the Hills today," she told Aerlich in the morning; and the silver stones under their feet as they left the barn lay silent. When the sheep were rounded up and moving, she set out in a direction that was not the direction she wished to go. They grazed that day across ground she had once often used, and it had grown almost lush—as lush as sheep-nibbled Hill-turf can ever grow—for its rest. Aerlich was as dutiful as ever, but he did look often over his shoulder as if to check that she was still there; and when he felt he had a minute free he would rush over to her, to press his jaw up against her legs and gaze adoringly into her face—and then dash off again, back to his flock. She couldn't eat her noon meal, and her hands shook, and she found herself irrationally annoyed that Aerlich no longer expected her to have anything to do with herding sheep.

. . . but the tears on her face were her own.

The second day was the same, except that the call to climb into the Hills was stronger; and on the third day she answered it. Aerlich understood at once as she chose the path that led them away from their once-familiar trails, and his head and tail drooped, though he kept the sheep no less snugly together for it.

Fel was sitting on a rock, waiting, as he had waited so many other days. He did not ask her where she had been; he gave her no words of reproach, but looking into his smooth, undisturbed face, she knew he had none to give. Their day together was shadowed, for her, by this knowledge, and before they parted that evening she took his face between her hands and stared long at him, at the strong straight nose, the curl of the black eyelashes. "The gods save me," she said hopelessly. "I love you." Fel did not reply, and she turned away, to follow her sheep.

SHE DID NOT GO into the Hills again. After the first few days she found it difficult to sleep, for she heard that call—whatever it was—even at night, and she trembled, and thrashed under her blanket, and her head ached, and in the morning her eyes were heavy. The call became something that she oriented herself by: it told her where not to go; it reminded her why she felt so awful all the time; it gave her suddenly empty life meaning by its existence. She dreamed no more of Donal, and she managed to be interested when the family received Ifgold's first letter. His journey had been uneventful; he was finding his feet with his peers, a few of whom were from even as vast a sweep of nowhere as himself; the masters were kind but the work was appalling. "Appalling" was his word, but it was obvious that he was delighted with it.

She held the letter in her hands to read it over to herself, after Thassie had read it aloud to everyone, and the memory of Ifgold and their friendship was very strong; he wrote just the way he talked, and she could hear him, and she missed him. She was free of the Hill call, for a moment, as she remembered her brother.

She wrote back. He answered almost at once, a letter just for her, although Igard and Lonnie nagged her into reading it aloud to everyone; and Ifgold must have guessed they would, for he said nothing that she need disguise. At the same time the relief in him was written larger than any of the words on the page, even as he spoke of harmless things, the work he was set, a boy he grew to be friends with. She read the letter several times. Her hands did not shake so much as they had.

SHE STILL COULD NOT SLEEP a night through; she still heard the call to come into the Hills, to leave her foolish sheep and her humorless dog and her dull family, and come to the Hills. She thought the call said *forever*. She thought: if he truly wanted me, he would come for me, and she squeezed her eyes shut.

He did not come, and the silver stones by the barn grew grey with use.

IT CAME EASIER as the weeks passed, and the seasons turned again; and she no longer burnt the food she cooked, and she was very rarely home late, and then only for a very good reason. The rest of the lambs were sold, and as everyone's flocks this year were short, she got a good price for them, and did not lose so much as she had feared; and this time she bargained hard. The sheep lost their skittishness around her, except insofar as sheep are always skittish, and occasionally she took tinder and flint with her, and food to cook, and had a hot meal in the lee of a boulder, and shared it with Aerlich, who began occasionally to let her make decisions about the sheep again. When she thought of Fel she thought only to wonder why what had happened had happened at all; and if the call still came from the Hills, she ignored it, as she learned to ignore a certain place beneath her breastbone, which had once not been empty, and now was.

A full year came round, and Donal came home. He came to her first, even before his family. They'd written few letters in the past year; that had been part of their agreement, that neither would feel slighted while each was buried in work, in earning the money for their life together. She had found it only too easy to write rarely, and then in haste, and briefly, about sheep and weather; and she could not have said, beyond the very first ones, what Donal's letters to her had contained. But he had written that he was coming; and, almost against her will, she felt a rising excitement as the last few days of their long separation passed. She woke up in the mornings almost happy, and she recognized the sense of expectancy before she remembered why she felt it; and in the resultant storm of conflicting emotions

. . . she thought only to wonder why . . .

she finally tried only to put all of it out of her mind. But it wouldn't leave her; and Donal was coming home.

She heard unfamiliar hoofbeats in the yard early one evening, and knew who it must be; and her mind had no part in the decision, for her feet picked her up and flung her out the door. Donal hugged her hard and then lifted her and swung her round.

"You're thinner," he said, just as she breathlessly said, "You're stronger." They were both right. Donal had never been burly, but a year's hard labor had filled him out, neck, chest, shoulders, and thighs; it was as if the old Donal had a new shadow. She looked at him a little fearfully, for he suddenly reminded her of someone else, someone who no longer existed for her; and she grabbed at his newly broad upper arms to steady herself, and stared into his face; he was very little taller than she. He looked back at her, puzzled and then hurt by her expression. "Aren't you happy to see me?"

"Of course I am," she said, and threw her arms around his neck and kissed him, and his arms closed eagerly around her. When he let her go she looked into his face again, and cupped her hands around it; his hair was brown, and his eyes brown too, warm against the black pupil, and his skin was a warm ruddy brown from the sun. She felt her face relax, and more easily she slipped back into his arms, and kissed him again, and his mouth smiled against hers.

When they turned, the rest of the family had come out, and Thassie had Lonnie's shoulder in a firm grip and gave her a shake as she was inclined to snigger. Kitchet had already gone to pet Donal's horse; they were having a low snuffly conversation off to one side.

Maddy's eye met her mother's, and a little hard look went between them; and Maddy snuggled against Donal's side and put her arm around his waist, and Thassie smiled.

Donal refused to be parted from her, and so swept her off with him to visit his parents. Her family sent her with him willingly—a little too willingly, she thought, but she did not pursue it. Everyone treats me like a convalescent, she thought more than once: they welcome me back as if from the gates of death, after an illness they had despaired of. The thought was bitter, and mixed of several bitternesses. And Donal, she saw, watched her anxiously when he thought she did not see; and she wondered if perhaps her mother had said something to him, but decided it was unlikely. Thassie was too grateful that her strayed daughter looked like she was coming back to the fold to risk the coming back by unnecessary words about the straying. And little does she know the truth of it, her daughter thought grimly.

But Maddy's determination to behave as she should, as if what had happened had not happened, or had not mattered, held her in good stead till she found that Donal's kindness, and obvious pleasure in her company, began truly to bring her back to what she once had been. She did not ask him what he guessed, and tried to pass it off lightly when he too treated her as gently as a recent invalid, and teased him that they had only been parted for a year—really, she was still Maddy. He searched her face with his eyes—and at night, when they lay together, with his lips and fingers—hoping to find the truth of her words; she did not know if he thought he had succeeded.

They were gone to his family a fortnight. Maddy had not argued when Donal insisted that she go with him, only arranged that Lonnie and Kitchet should go together with Aerlich and the sheep; not that Aerlich needed human companions, particularly not young, almost useless ones, but even Lonnie should enjoy a break from her usual farm chores, and Kitchet idolized her biggest sister, and was delighted to get to do what Maddy did.

Kitchet was full of the wonders of sheep-grazing when they got back: the views from her favorite hillsides, the cleverness of Aerlich, the personalities of sheep. "Personalities!" Maddy said, laughing. "You give them more credit than I ever have. Well! You will grow up to be our next shepherd. I'm glad. I agree, wandering alone over the Hills is like nothing else. . . ." Her voice trailed off, and the adults grew very still; but Lonnie said in her blunt way, "It's *boring*. Nothing but rocks and scrub and more rocks and scrub, and sheep are stupid and they smell, and Aerlich does everything." Everyone laughed, and the tension was blown away.

And then at last she and Donal went off to look at their farmsite. She had wheedled him into staying an extra day with her family— their chosen valley was less than a day's brisk march from her mother's farm—saying that the weather promised rain, and she didn't want to come trailing into their new home dripping wet and miserable. Donal laughed and agreed to wait. They spent one cloudy day on a little knoll close enough to her mother's farm to look down on the buildings from where they sat watching the sheep. Aerlich seemed exhausted, and let Maddy do more of the work than he had since . . . she stopped the thought abruptly. But it didn't rain, and on the next

". . . and Aerlich does everything."

day dawn arrived with a glad blue sky, and she had no further excuses, though a sense of oppression weighed her spirit more and more.

But she put a bright face on it and after a quick breakfast she and Donal set out. At the last minute she decided to take Aerlich too. The sheep would be content in their small outdoor pen, with plenty of silage; and she awarded Kitchet the task of keeping an eye on them. She and Donal would return the next day.

Aerlich was suprised when she whistled him away from the sheep pen. He looked at her, and he looked at the sheep, nosing through their fodder, rubbing along the fence for splintery spots that might catch at their fleece so they could bolt away in terror, and running blindly into one another so that they could complain about it—and the weight on her spirit lifted long enough to let her laugh at him. "Come along, silly," she said. "It's a holiday."

He stiffened all over and turned his face away because she'd called him silly, and she smiled, and the oppression lifted a little more, because she remembered the days when he had treated her humorlessly, as a burden. She said gently, "Come, Aerlich," and he came.

But he didn't seem to know what to do with himself, and for most of the day kept close to Maddy's heels, bumping into her if she stopped suddenly. But she was almost as dumbly following Donal, who strode out confidently. He called over his shoulder sometimes about this bird, "I haven't seen one of those in a year!" or that fall of rock, "Isn't it ever going to fall down the rest of the way?" or general cheerful nothings she didn't bother to hear. For her own breath came short, and the Hills, her Hills, gave her no joy, neither the rock and

". . . the next day dawn arrived with a glad blue sky . . ."

turf underfoot nor the bird-speckled sky overhead; nor the rough green smell of the hardy Hill-grass and the low sturdy trees; and she knew at last some measure of her real loss, and the reason her heart beat so hollowly.

She hurried Donal on when he would have stopped for lunch, and he fell in with her haste willingly, misinterpreting it as eagerness to reach the end of their journey. But when they came down over the little rocky shoulder that heralded the gap in the Hill's side that gave into their valley, her feet slowed involuntarily, and Donal went on alone. He was out of sight around the spur when he missed her; but as he turned back to call she came round it herself and stood beside him.

There was grass in their valley, real grass, and a few real trees, for the Hill curved around it on three sides, and the entrance to it was southwest. It was sheltered from the bitter winter wind, and from the irresponsible summer wind that sometimes knocked down half-grown crops and scoured the thin topsoil away from the rock that always lay near beneath the earth of the Hills. A little stream watered it, and spread out to become a pool before it parted again into several rivulets that ran in all directions; it had been a joke in her family that this tiny lake fed the stream that ran near her mother's farm, and that she would be able to send messages, once she and Donal had made their own farm beside it, by wrapping notes around stones and dropping them in the water. Kitchet—very young then—had believed it.

She looked at her valley, at its green spring promise of the fulfillment of her and Donal's dreams, at everything they had worked for the last six years, and she burst into tears. Donal said, "My own darling, whatever is wrong?" But he saw at once that she was beyond speech, and so took her in his arms and rocked her gently, while she held on to him as she might a tree in a storm; and Aerlich sat at their feet and whined, a tiny, anxious, high-pitched whine.

She quieted at last, and they walked hand in hand to the pool where she washed her face—and gasped, for it was brutally cold—and then they sat down together, and he put an arm around her and she rested her tired head on his shoulder and gave a long shuddering sigh. The tears seemed to have washed away her ability to think; what could she say? She was not sure she could explain anything satisfactorily even to herself; so what could she say to Donal, when there was so much she could not say to him, and would not say to herself?

"I can't stay here," she said at last, dully, and there was a silence, and Aerlich put his head on her leg and looked up at her.

"I—I think I have guessed that much," Donal said. "I—perhaps I guessed it some time ago." There was something in his voice she could not identify.

"I'm sorry."

His shoulder lifted briefly under her cheek. "This valley was always more yours than mine. I only want to farm. It's you who has Hillrock for bones."

"We could go somewhere else," she said tentatively; and he caught her up at once, sharply: *"We?"*

Then she knew what she heard in his voice: fear. His *we* hung in the air between them, as cold as the mountain water, and she said, "If—if you wish to come with me," and heard fear in her own voice.

He sighed, and his breath caught in his chest halfway. "I do wish it. Perhaps I wish it as desperately as you wish not to stay here. . . . I'm sorry. I thought you loved the Hills best of all; better than me, better certainly than your sheep, which I've always believed were only an excuse to let you run free up here. I want to farm—somewhere—and I want you, and I don't—I don't want to have to choose between you."

She said, muffled by his shoulder, "My brother has written of the land around his school; he can't altogether stop being a farmer for all he's a scholar now. He says it's good land, rich, and under-used." She heard her voice speaking, as if from very far away; it sounded vague and unconvincing. She remembered Ifgold's words in his letter, and wondered if he had written them just for this occasion. She remembered, from even longer ago, the tales that many of the local farmers told about the southlands; how, very far away, farther even than Ifgold's school, there were orange groves. But she had heard the tales with indifference, and remembered them little; for she had Hillrock for bones. "He says they've only begun to learn to irrigate, but . . ."

Donal laughed. "If it weren't for you I would never have thought of staying in the Hills. It's wild land here—not farmland. But I was afraid to say anything. Afraid that you'd decide I was too dull and ordinary a fellow, too tame, for you and your Hills. . . . This valley would have been fine," he went on hastily. "There is some real earth here. But south, to Illya, where your brother is—to grow something besides korf and a few vegetables! Yes, I should like it above all things. I'm sorry. If I'd known—if I'd guessed—I'd have spoken long ago."

She looked up into his face, transformed with happiness, and a new little glow began to bloom in her own heart, and she realized

. . . and a new little glow began to bloom . . .

that he would be tender with her always about his mistake; and that since she would for long need the tenderness she would let him go on thinking the mistake was his.

"We can set out as soon as you like," he went on, eagerly. "We'll not need to take much with us; it will make better sense to start fresh when we arrive."

"I'll write Ifgold, so that he can look us out a place to stay," she said slowly, and her voice sounded less hollow, and she smiled timidly at Donal. "He lives in a boardinghouse near the school; perhaps there's even room there, while we look around us."

After a moment she went on, "I'll sell the rest of my damn sheep; Kitchet can start her own flock if she wants to, when she's old enough."

"The sheep are your problem," Donal said firmly. "I refuse to have anything to do with anything that doesn't have roots and isn't green."

Maddy was suddenly conscious of the weight across her leg, and she looked down into a black-and-white face with hopeful brown eyes. "Aerlich will come with us. If we decide—if I decide—not to have sheep, I'll buy him some geese to herd."